ROBO-
RUNNERS
Razorbites

Books in the **Robo-Runners** series:

The Tin Man

Tunnel Racers

Razorbites

Powerball

The Ghost Sea

Aquanauts

by DAMIAN HARVEY

Illustrated by Mark Oliver

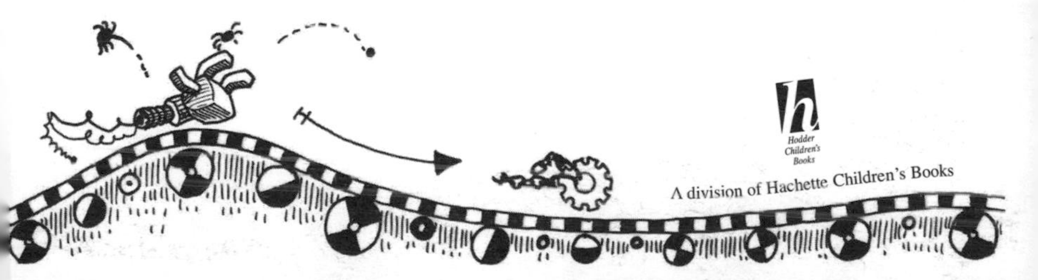

First published in Great Britain in 2008
by Hodder Children's Books
This paperback edition published 2009

1

A Catalogue record for this book is available from the British Library

ISBN-13: 978 0 340 94488 2

Printed and bound in Great Britain by Clays Ltd, St Ives plc

Hodder Children's Books
A division of Hachette Children's Books
338 Euston Road, London NW1 3BH
An Hachette Livre UK Company

For Craig with love

1

The Wastelands stretch from the walls of Metrocity and its sprawling junk yard, all the way to the Mountains of Khan on the far horizon.

Dry riverbeds snake their way into the distance and the bones of creatures long since dead litter the ground. Nothing lives in the Wastelands for very long.

Into this land of dust, heat and bones came four robot friends, Crank, Al, Torch and Grunt, travelling in search of a safe place for old robots.

A place where robots can be free to live their lives in peace.

A place called Robotika.

The red and black tunnel racer they were riding on tore across the sun-baked ground, crushing dried bones and throwing up clouds of dust with its tyres as it left Metrocity and the junk yard far behind.

"Look out!" shouted Torch, the old Fire and Rescue robot, as he clung to the top of the racer.

The remains of an old spaceship, lying half buried in the dusty ground, jutted into the air a little way ahead of them.

"Don't worry," shouted Crank, gripping the steering wheel. "I've seen it."

The racer's engine let out a roar as Crank pressed his foot down on the accelerator and headed straight for the old spaceship.

"Hold tight," he yelled, "we're going over the top."

"Nooooo!" cried Al, desperately trying to find something to hold on to as the front wheels of the racer hit the top of the spaceship.

"Arghhhhhh," screamed Al and Torch as the racer ran up the spaceship's sloping roof.

"Yaaaaaah – poooooo," yelled Crank, as the racer shot over the edge and flew through the air.

"Hur, hur, hur," laughed Grunt as the racer hit the ground with a heavy crunch and sped off across the Wastelands.

"You must be mad," cried Torch. "You could have wrecked the racer."

"You could have wrecked *us*," shouted Al.

"Again," laughed Grunt. "Grunt want to do it again."

"No," said Crank, shaking his head. "We'd better not. Torch and Al are right. It could damage the racer, and we don't want to do that."

"That is right," said Al. "In a racer like this we could reach Robotika in no time at all."

"No we couldn't," said Grunt.

"Of course we could," said Al. "Just look how fast we are going."

"Nah!" said Grunt, shaking his head again. "Grunt finks we will soon run out of fuel."

"What?" cried Crank, looking at the fuel gauge in disbelief.

Grunt was right. The tunnel racer would run out of fuel very soon. It was almost on empty now.

"What happens when we run out of fuel?" asked Al.

"We stop," said Grunt.

"I know that," said Al. "I mean what happens to us?"

"Oh," said Grunt. "Dat is easy … We will be stranded in da Wastelands with nowhere to go. Da sun will go down and da scavengers will come out."

"Then what?" asked Crank, looking worried.

"Oh! I know, I know," said Torch, waving his arm in the air excitedly. "We'll try and get away but the scavengers will hunt us down and tear us apart."

"Dat is right," said Grunt, nodding his head.

"But that is terrible," said Al. "We have not come all this way just to get torn apart by scavengers."

"Al's right," said Crank. "There must be *something* we can do. We just need to get more fuel for the tunnel racer. There *must* be a fuel station around here somewhere?"

"Oh yeah," said Grunt, pointing off into the distance with one huge hand. "Dare it is."

"Where?" said Crank, peering round. "I can't see a fuel station."

"Dat's coz dare isn't one," said Grunt, shaking his head. "We is in da Wastelands, remember ... Dare is just miles and miles of dust ... and rocks ... and bones. Dare is nothing else."

"Oh yes there is," said Al, balancing on one hand as he pointed into the distance with the other. "There is a big cloud of dust."

The others turned to see where Al was looking, and sure enough, a big cloud of dust could be seen rising into the air in the distance. Crank brought the red and black tunnel racer to a skidding halt so they could get a better look at the dust cloud.

"What is it?" said Crank, wriggling out of his seat.

"I do not know," said Al. "It is hard to see from down here. If someone lifts me up I am sure to get a better view, after all, my eyesight *is* very good. I was fitted with the latest SPX3 visual sensors. They are top of the range robotic eyes."

Ever since the Tin Man had stolen his legs in the recycling plant, Al had been forced to walk round on his hands. They'd gone through the junk yard and the Mekanix Workshop, but still hadn't found any replacement legs for him.

But despite this, Al still managed to remind his friends that he was a brand new "top of the range" robot and that being sent to the recycling plant had all been a big mistake.

Grunt picked Al up in his huge hands and held him high above his head.

"Dare," said Grunt. "What do you see?"

The three robots waited in hopeful silence as Al stared out into the distance with his SPX3, top of the range robot eyes.

"Yes," said Al, nodding his head. "I thought so..."

"What is it?" cried Crank. "What is it?"

"It is a big cloud of dust," said Al.

"We know that," said Crank. "But what's making it?"

"I do not know," said Al. "It is much too far away."

"It could be anyfink," said Grunt. "Grunt fink it's probably just scavengers."

"I don't think so," said Torch, who was still staring at the dust cloud. "It looks like a convoy of

land cruisers to me. If you stare long enough you can just make them out through the dust."

"Land cruisers!" said Al. "We are saved."

"Saved?" said Crank.

"Of course," said Al. "Perhaps they have fuel, and perhaps they will let us have some."

"And *perhaps* they *are* scavengers," said Crank. "And *perhaps* they'll pull us apart for scrap."

"Crank's right," said Torch. "But I don't think we have much choice. We can't stay out here in the Wastelands."

As Crank clambered back into the tunnel racer's seat the others jumped aboard and held on tight. Crank pressed his foot down on the accelerator and the racer roared off towards the big cloud of dust that was rising from the convoy of land cruisers in the distance.

The four robot friends were so busy looking forwards that none of them saw the small cloud of dust that rose from something following them in the distance. Something that had been following ever since they'd escaped from the junk yard.

As the red and black racer bounced across dried riverbeds and rolled its way across the dusty ground of the Wastelands, the distant convoy of land cruisers got steadily closer.

"Look at them," said Crank. "I've never seen so many old land cruisers before."

The convoy was made up of land cruisers of different shapes and sizes.

Some were big transporters, used to haul heavy cargo from city to city, while others were much smaller, family-sized land cruisers that would only seat three or four people at the most.

The convoy moved across the Wastelands on a mixture of wheels and caterpillar tracks. Some of the more modern land cruisers had anti-gravity hover drives which allowed them to float a little way above the dusty ground, but a couple didn't seem capable of moving at all and were being dragged along with thick tow-chains.

"They look a right mess," said Crank, easing

his foot off the accelerator pedal and letting the racer slow down.

"They look beautiful," said Al. "We *are* saved."

"I'm not so sure about that," said Torch. "Something doesn't quite look right to me … But I'm not sure what it is."

"Grunt finks we is about to find out," said Grunt. "Dey is coming."

One of the smaller land cruisers had broken away from the rest of the convoy and was skimming its way across the dusty ground towards the four friends.

"It's about time too," said Crank. "I think we're out of fuel."

No sooner had he said this than the racer's engine spluttered and coughed a couple of times then came to a complete stop. Without its huge engine to power it, the red and black racer ground to a halt.

Crank was clambering out of the driver's seat as the small land cruiser reached them and came to a stop, hovering a short distance away.

"Hello," shouted Al. "We seem to have broken down. I wonder if you could help us?"

There was no reply from the land cruiser. It just hovered in front of them, its anti-gravity drive making the dust dance and spin beneath it. The four robot friends tried to peer inside but there was nothing to be seen as the windscreen was dark and covered in dust, though there must have been someone or something at the controls.

"How rude," said Al. "I am sure they must have heard me."

"I'm sure they have," said Torch. "We'll just have to be patient. After all, they don't know who we are. They could be frightened of us."

"Frightened," laughed Crank. "Why would anyone be frightened of us?"

"Yeah," growled Grunt, scratching his head with a hand the size of a shovel. "We is not frightening."

"Hmm," said Crank thoughtfully, looking at Grunt for a moment.

Many years ago, Grunt had worked in Metrocity's junk yard and had used his huge hands and amazing strength to move piles of scrap metal around. Grunt was a big robot … a robot big enough and strong enough to crush a small land cruiser without much difficulty.

"Perhaps Torch has a point," said Crank. "Some of us might look a little bit frightening."

"Nah," said Grunt. "We is nice robots." And to prove it, Grunt waved one of his giant hands and smiled as nicely as he could, baring his huge teeth … huge teeth that had been designed to tear through scrap metal.

There was a loud whine from the land cruiser and it suddenly flew forwards and shot past the side of the racer.

"Oh, well done!" said Al. "You have really frightened them off now."

"Grunt didn't do nuffink," said Grunt. "I only smiled at dem."

"Well, never mind," said Crank, "I guess we walk from here."

Crank was about to jump down from the racer when the land cruiser flew past again, this time heading back towards the convoy. As it went by there was a loud popping sound and something flew out behind it.

"Duck," cried Crank, "they're firing at us!"

Crank threw himself to one side and landed face first on the dusty ground as something heavy hit the front of the racer close to where he'd been standing.

"Did you see that?" yelled Crank. "They're trying to kill us."

"No they're not," said Torch. "It's a magnetic tow cable. You'd better get back on before we—aargh!"

Before Torch had a chance to finish what he was saying,

the racer jolted forwards sending him, Al and Grunt sprawling on to their backs. Luckily, none of them fell off the top of the racer and they all managed to find something to hold on to as the little land cruiser began pulling them towards the convoy.

"Wait for me!" yelled Crank, getting to his feet.

"I think you will have to run," said Al. "It does not look as though they are going to wait."

For once, Crank didn't argue. The land cruiser was picking up speed as it towed the racer, and it was getting further away by the second. If he didn't catch up with his friends soon he'd find himself all alone in the Wastelands.

Crank wasn't sure what would happen when they reached the convoy but he did know one thing … he'd never be able to find Robotika on his own.

There was only one thing for it. He would have to run.

Chasing the red and black racer across the Wastelands, Crank wished he'd got Al to repair his leg properly when there'd been a chance. When they'd first arrived at the recycling plant, Al had accidentally pulled one of Crank's legs off, and although he'd fixed it back on he had somehow managed to put it the wrong way round.

For most of the time, having one foot facing backwards didn't cause Crank much of a problem ... but running across the Wastelands was a different matter and Crank found himself stumbling over rocks and dried bones. He even fell flat on his face several times after catching his foot in cracks and holes in the dry ground.

"Come on, Crank," yelled Torch, leaning over the back of the racer and reaching out towards his friend. "Grab my hand."

Crank reached forwards as he got closer. Faster and faster he went until the tips of his fingers touched Torch's outstretched hand.

"That's it," yelled Torch. "I've nearly got you!"

Crank put on a final burst of speed, running so fast he felt sure his joints would come apart. And just as he started to think that he wasn't going to make it, Torch grabbed his hand.

"Got you!" yelled Torch.

Crank opened his mouth to reply, but as he did so, his foot caught on a rock and sent him sprawling into the air.

"Arghh!" Crank cried, flying forwards. He tried to grab the back of the racer with his free hand but there was nothing to hold on to and he found himself dropping to the floor.

"Hold on," yelled Torch.

"I am holding on," shouted Crank, as he was dragged along behind the racer.

"You'll have to pull me up."

Still gripping Crank's hand as tightly as he could, Torch tried to pull him to safety but found *himself* slipping off the back of the racer.

"I'm falling," yelled Torch.

"Oh no you isn't," said Grunt, as he grabbed Torch's legs and started pulling him back on top of the racer. As Grunt was dragging him back, Torch closed his eyes and concentrated on keeping a tight hold on Crank's hand.

"Don't worry," yelled Torch. "We've got you."

"Dare," said Grunt. "Dat woz a close one … Hey! What is you doing wiv Crank's arm?"

Still holding Crank's hand as tightly as he could, Torch opened his eyes and looked up.

"What are you talking about?" he said.

But Torch didn't need telling … He could see for himself.

Although he hadn't lost his grip on Crank's hand, Torch *had* lost Crank.

Crank definitely wasn't on top of the racer and he wasn't being dragged behind it any more either. There was just Crank's arm lying there where the rest of him should have been. There were a couple of wires sticking out from the end of the arm but there was definitely no Crank.

"Oh dear," said Al. "Crank is not going to like that one bit. You should have seen how cross he got when I pulled his leg off."

"You is right," said Grunt. "He does not look happy at all."

Looking behind them, Torch, Al and Grunt could see Crank had wasted no time at all. He was already up on his feet and running after them … and he didn't look very happy.

"I was just holding on to his hand," said Torch. "It's not my fault his arm fell off."

"Do not worry," said Al. "You can give it back to him in a moment. Crank seems to be catching up with us."

"It's amazing how fast he can run," said Torch. "Especially for such an old robot."

"He isn't dat fast," said Grunt, miserably. "My little Scamp could run as fast as dat."

Scamp had been Grunt's pet botweiler and this was the first time he'd mentioned the robo-dog since leaving the junk yard. Torch and Al knew only too well how fast botweilers could run as one had chased them through the junk yard. They'd been lucky Grunt and Scamp had been there to rescue them, and although Scamp had seemed friendly enough, the very thought of botweilers made Torch and Al shudder.

"Don't worry," said Torch. "I'm sure Scamp is much happier in the junk yard than he would have been out here in the Wastelands."

"Anyway," said Al, "Crank is not running very fast at all. *We* are slowing down."

Al was right. They had caught up with the convoy and were slowing down.

From a distance, Crank had thought the convoy looked a mess, but now they were closer they could see just how much of a mess it really was. A lot of the old cruisers seemed to have been repaired using big pieces of scrap metal taken from old spacecraft. Some of them had odd bits and pieces added to them that you wouldn't normally find on a land cruiser. Nets, cranes and a strange array of ancient weaponry.

As the cruiser that was towing them approached the rest of the convoy, one of the bigger vehicles moved out of line and stopped alongside them.

It was then that Crank finally caught up with his friends.

"Well thanks for waiting," said Crank.

"There was nothing we could do," said Torch. "They wouldn't stop."

"I bet they wouldn't," said Crank,

grumpily snatching his broken arm back off him. "I'll have this back if you don't mind."

"Would you like me to fix it for you?" asked Al.

"No thanks," said Crank, huffily. "I can fix it myself."

Crank was just snapping his arm back into place when a loud voice shouted at them.

"YOU WILL ALL STAND STILL."

"How rude," said Al.

"SILENCE!" roared the voice.

The four friends looked at the big land cruiser, trying to work out where the voice was coming from, when a large robot appeared high up on the roof.

It was one of the biggest robots Crank had seen, even bigger than Grunt. It was also one of the most ridiculous-looking robots Crank had ever seen. It had a tiny head and a huge body. And as if that wasn't bad enough, the robot had been painted to make it look as though it was wearing clothes.

Not just any old clothes either ... this robot looked as though it was wearing a black suit and a bow-tie.

In one swift movement, the big robot leaped down from the top of the land cruiser and landed on the ground in front of the four friends.

"You tin-heads are in for a treat," sneered the big robot. "You're going to meet Quill."

"Who's he callin' tin-heads," growled Grunt. "I should punch 'is lights out."

"Not now," whispered Torch. "We have to be polite ... we *do* need their help."

"SILENCE!" roared the big robot, glaring at Torch. "Quill is here."

A door opened in the side of the land cruiser and Quill stepped out on to the ground, his boots kicking up dust with every step that he took.

Al noticed the boots straight away because they were so odd. While one of them was smart and black, the other was scruffy, brown, and seemed about four sizes too big.

Torch hadn't noticed the odd boots at all. He was too busy staring at Quill's coat. He'd heard stories about people wearing fur coats but had never expected to see one for himself. It had been illegal to hunt animals for many years now and the only fur coats to be seen were found in museums.

Quill's coat looked ancient, though Torch didn't think any museums would be interested in it. The fur itself was filthy, matted with dirt and grime, and one of the sleeves had been completely torn off, revealing a thin, bare arm.

There was something else about the coat that bothered Torch but he couldn't quite put his finger on what it was until Quill got closer ... then it came to him.

Although the animal that had once owned the fur had been dead for a very long time, the coat itself was still full of life. It was crawling with bugs and flies. Torch could see them weaving their way through the filthy fur, some of them disappearing into the armhole or clambering over the collar.

Creepy-crawlies didn't usually bother robots as there was nothing much for them to bite, but the sight of them wriggling around on Quill's coat made Torch's circuits shudder.

As Quill walked towards them he scratched at his neck a couple of times, but apart from that, the mass of crawling bugs didn't seem to bother him. Torch thought that was very strange because there was something about Quill that had come as a surprise to him and his friends.

"*It's a softy!*" said Grunt with amazement. "Grunt can't remember the last time he saw a softy."

"They prefer to be called *humans*," whispered Torch.

"SILENCE!" roared the big robot. "Quill will speak."

"Thank you," said Quill, smiling at the four friends. "I see you've already met Bouncer."

"Bouncer?" said Crank.

"Yeah!" sneered the big robot. "Bouncer! That's because I like to bounce on little robots like you lot."

"Who's he callin' little," growled Grunt. "I should really punch 'is lights out."

"Not now," said Torch. "We're being polite, remember."

"Quite right," said Quill, with a smile. "We should all be polite, shouldn't we, Bouncer?"

"If you say so, boss," said Bouncer. "But I think this lot will be trouble."

"Trouble?" said Al. "We are never any trouble. We've just run out of fuel and need a little help to get going."

"There you are, Bouncer," said Quill. "They'll be no trouble at all."

"Does that mean you can help?" asked Al.

"Of course we can help," said Quill. "We're always happy to help robots in trouble. Isn't that right, Bouncer?"

"Oh yes," sneered Bouncer. "We always like to help poor little robots in trouble."

"That's great," said Crank. "We're glad to hear it. So if you could just let us have a bit of fuel we'll be on our way."

"Fuel?" said Quill, scratching his neck. "Now that's where we have a problem. Isn't that right, Bouncer?"

"Oh yes," said Bouncer. "Fuel is a *big* problem out here on the Wastelands. That's why we have a *big* fuel tanker."

"A fuel tanker!" said Al excitedly. "That is great."

"It is great," said Quill, frowning at Bouncer. "But *sadly*, our tanker is empty."

"WHAT!" cried Bouncer. "But I checked it before and it was—"

"I said the tanker is EMPTY," repeated Quill, with a frown. "Isn't that right, Bouncer?"

The big robot's face looked blank for a moment as it thought about what Quill had said. Then its familiar sneer returned as it nodded its head.

"Oh yeah," said Bouncer. "I must have forgotten. Our tanker *is* empty."

"That's right," said Quill. "But don't you worry. You can travel with us to the coliseum. Perhaps you can get fuel there."

"You're going to the coliseum?" said Torch. "I've always wanted to go and see the coliseum, but I thought it was empty now."

"It is usually," said Quill. "But we're going to be putting on a *special show* so there will be lots of people there. Isn't that right, Bouncer?"

"Oh yes, Quill," said Bouncer. "Lots of people come to see our *special show*."

"A show?" said Crank. "Are you like a travelling circus or something?"

"I suppose we are," said Quill with a smile. "*Something* like a travelling circus."

"That's great!" said Crank. "I've always wanted to see a circus."

"That's settled then," said Quill. "You're coming to the coliseum ... and who knows, you might even be in the show yourself."

"Oh no," said Crank. "I could never be in a circus."

"You never know what's going to happen," said Quill. "Isn't that right, Bouncer?"

"Oh yes," said Bouncer, grinning. "That is right. They don't know what's going to happen, do they?"

Quill smiled and disappeared back into the land cruiser, leaving Bouncer alone with the four friends.

"You lot better stay on your little car until we get to the coliseum," he sneered. "Be careful you don't

fall off though. We wouldn't want you hurting yourselves, would we?"

Bouncer unhooked a length of thick chain from the back of the big land cruiser and fastened it to the front of the tunnel racer with a rusty hook.

"Watch what you is doin'," growled Grunt. "You is goin' to scratch the paintwork."

"Ha!" laughed Bouncer, giving the racer a kick.

"You'll have more than that to worry about soon enough."

Then, with a single jump, Bouncer leaped into the air, landed on top of the big land cruiser and disappeared from view. The four friends were left to clamber back on the tunnel racer as the land cruiser moved off with the rest of the convoy, pulling them behind it.

As they were towed into line with the other land cruisers, Crank, Al and Torch couldn't help thinking about the way Quill had smiled at them. There was something about all this that made them wonder whether going along with the convoy was a good idea, but for now they didn't have much choice. With the tunnel racer out of fuel they'd be forced to walk … and the Wastelands were not a nice place to go walking.

Grunt wondered how much longer they were going to have to be nice because he really did want to punch Bouncer's lights out.

As they sped across the Wastelands with the convoy there was nothing for the four robot friends to do other than sit and watch the scenery rolling by. On one side, mile after mile of dusty desert stretched to the horizon, while on the other the Mountains of Khan rose like a huge wall, dark and brooding.

"Dis is boring," complained Grunt.

Crank was lying on his back with his arms behind his head. "Why don't you relax for a while?" he said. "Catch some sun."

"Catch some sun?" said Grunt, sounding puzzled. "How can you catch some sun?"

"I don't really know," admitted Crank, "but I saw humans doing it once on a vid-screen."

"Sounds stupid to me," said Grunt. "Dem softies is crazy."

"Well it's better than complaining all the time," said Crank. "There's nothing we can do until we get to the coliseum, is there?"

"Well Grunt don't like just sittin' here waitin'," said Grunt. "Grunt don't trust dat Bouncer or his boss, Quill."

"I don't trust them either," agreed Torch. "There's something they're not telling us, but we haven't got much choice.

We won't get far without fuel and the coliseum seems to be the only place where we can get some."

"Grunt finks dey ave loads of fuel in dat tanker," said Grunt, looking back at the rest of the convoy. "Dey just don't want us to have any."

"I'm sure you're right," said Crank, "but we can't do much about that either, can we?"

"Perhaps we could borrow some fuel without dem knowing," suggested Grunt, with a mischievous smile.

"I do not think that would be a good idea at all," said Al. "And I am sure Mr Quill would not be happy about it either."

"Ha," laughed Grunt. "What can he do about it?"

"I do not know," said Al. "But I do not want to find out. We could end up in big trouble."

"Grunt finks we is already in big trouble," said Grunt. "We just don't know what it is yet."

"Why don't we have a look round?" suggested Torch. "It would be easy enough to climb on to this big land cruiser in front."

"Bouncer is sure to see you," said Al. "And we do not want to make him angry. I do not think he likes us anyway."

"Grunt isn't frightened of Bouncer," said Grunt. "I could squash him with one hand."

"I'm sure you could," said Torch, "but Al's right. We don't want to upset Bouncer as I'm sure he'd like nothing better than to leave us stranded in the Wastelands."

"HEY!" yelled a voice from above. "What are you up to?"

The four friends looked up and saw Bouncer standing on top of the big land cruiser in front of them.

"You don't fink he heard us, do you?" whispered Grunt.

"I hope not," said Torch. "He's certainly keeping

his eye on us though. We'll have to be careful."

"The convoy will be slowing down soon to cross the Great River," said Bouncer. "But don't get off your little car or you'll get left behind ... and we wouldn't want that, would we?"

Bouncer sneered at the four robots and then disappeared from view.

"He *really* don't want us wanderin' round, does he?" said Grunt.

"No," agreed Torch. "I wonder what he's trying to hide?"

"I don't know," said Grunt, "but I'm gonna find out. I'm not sitting here any longer."

"No!" cried Al.

But it was too late. Grunt was already running along the top of the red and black racer towards the big land cruiser in front of them. He jumped over Crank and then leaped high into the air, reaching out to grab one of the chains that hung from the back of the cruiser.

No sooner had Grunt caught hold of the chain than the air was filled with the sounds of squealing brakes and whining engines. The convoy was slowing down.

"Come back," shouted Crank. "Something's happening."

"We are here!" cried Al. "This is so exciting … I have never seen the Great River before."

It was no surprise to hear Al had never seen the Great River. Being a new robot, he had never even set foot outside Metrocity before. Crank and the others had seen the Great River lots of times on vid-screens and in pictures. It was the biggest river on the whole planet, carrying millions of gallons of water across the plains and wastelands, all the way from the Mountains of Khan down to the ocean … But even they weren't prepared for the view that met their eyes as the convoy slowed down.

The ruins of what had once been a ticket office stood by the edge of the riverbank. Its roof had collapsed long ago and one of the walls had fallen out on to the remains of the old road. Years before, people would have driven along this road and bought their tickets before waiting for the ferry to take them to the other side.

Crank and the others soon realised it would be no good waiting for the ferry today. The rusted remains of the once-great boat lay half buried in the middle of the river. Sand had drifted up

on to its decks and there was a huge gaping hole in the hull.

Where the cool waters of the Great River had once flowed, there was now a wide expanse of dust and rock. It looked like it had been a long time since any water had run between these riverbanks.

"Well," said Al. "This is not what I expected at all."

"It's not what I expected either," said Crank. "Where's the Great River?"

"This is it," said Torch. "All that's left of it anyway."

The land cruiser rumbled down the riverbank and out across the dried riverbed, pulling the racer behind it. Through the hole in the boat's hull, gleaming eyes glared out from the darkness within.

"Scavengers," said Grunt, pointing at the glowing eyes as he clambered back down on to the racer.

Torch opened his mouth to reply but as he did so a loud explosion shook the air and a cloud of smoke rose up from further back along the convoy.

The four friends stood up and tried to see what was happening, but the land cruiser behind them was so close it blocked out most of the view.

Then there was a shout …

"STOP THEM!"

It was Quill. He was up on top of the land cruiser with Bouncer, pointing at something.

As Crank and the others turned to see what it was, three robots ran into view, tripping over rocks and stumbling in their effort to get across the dried riverbed.

One of the robots looked back at Crank and the others …

"RUN!" cried the robot. "Run for your lives."

Crank, Al, Torch and Grunt watched as the three robots tripped, stumbled and ran across the dried riverbed.

"Was dat robot talking to us?" asked Grunt.

"I don't know," said Torch.

"Why are they running?" asked Crank.

"I don't know that either," said Torch. "But I think we're about to find out ... Look!"

The roof of the land cruiser behind them had started to open and the four friends could see metal claws scratching around the edges of the opening. Something was trying to get out.

As the roof opened wider six insect-like robots shot out through the gap. They buzzed and rattled through the air before landing on the dusty ground where they flexed their arms and legs and snapped their steely claws.

"What on earth are they?" cried Crank.

"I've no idea," said Torch. "I've never seen anything like them before."

"They are Razorbites," Bouncer called, watching them from the top of the land cruiser. "Quill's little pets. Now watch them play."

Crank, Al, Torch and Grunt watched in horror as the six Razorbites leaped from rock to rock, buzzing and snapping their claws, chasing after the three robot runaways.

The three robots were going as fast as they could, bounding over rocks and jumping over dried pieces of wood, heading towards the wreck of the ferryboat that lay in the middle of the Great River.

As the friends watched, the robot closest to them tripped and fell to the floor. Two of the Razorbites were on it in an instant, tearing and ripping it apart as if it were an old tin can. Bits of the robot flew everywhere and the two Razorbites destroyed it in a matter of seconds before moving on to join the others in chasing the two remaining runaways.

The two robots had almost reached the wreck of the ferry when the Razorbites caught up with them. One quickly fell to the floor as five of the insect-like robot attackers pounced on it, but the last one carried on bravely for a few more yards, battling against a single Razorbite that had landed on its back.

For a moment it looked as though the third robot might get away. It had managed to throw its attacker to the floor and was off and running again. It leaped over a final rock then made a desperate jump for the opening in the side of the old ferryboat.

Whether the robot would have been safe inside the wrecked boat was never known. Before it managed to pull itself inside, three Razorbites crashed down on to it, sending it sprawling to the ground.

There was a scream, followed by the sound of tearing metal as the robot disappeared beneath a mass of snapping claws and teeth.

Crank, Al, Torch and Grunt stood in shocked silence for a moment, none of them knowing what to say.

"I'm sorry you had to see that," said Quill.

Crank and the others looked up to see Quill looking down at them from the top of the land cruiser.

"Who were those robots?" asked Al, still unable to take his eyes off the grisly scene in front of them.

"I should have told you about them before," said Quill. "They were prisoners. Isn't that right, Bouncer?"

"Oh yes, Quill," said Bouncer, nodding his head. "Very dangerous prisoners."

"Dangerous prisoners!" said Al. "What are you doing with dangerous prisoners?"

"We often find them wandering round the Wastelands," said Quill. "We pick them up and take them to the coliseum. Isn't that right, Bouncer?"

"Oh yes, Quill," agreed Bouncer. "We take good care of them."

"So why did you destroy them?" asked Torch.

"They were trying to escape," said Quill. "They'd damaged one of my land cruisers and destroyed two of my guards. They had to be stopped before they hurt anyone else."

Quill turned away from the four friends and clapped his hands three times.

Instantly, the six Razorbites raced back to the convoy and, with a buzzing and snapping of claws, disappeared inside the land cruiser behind them.

"Well that's the end of today's little show," said Quill. "I think we should get on with our journey, if you're all ready."

The four friends nodded their heads and Quill disappeared back into the land cruiser. In a few moments the convoy had crossed the dried riverbed and was moving off across the Wastelands once more and heading for the coliseum.

"It is no wonder they told us to stay here on the racer," said Al. "It would be dangerous to go wandering round in a convoy full of prisoners."

"I'm not so sure about that," said Torch. "Something still doesn't seem right to me."

"Grunt finks you is right," agreed Grunt. "So is we going to 'ave a look round now?"

"No," said Torch. "We've seen what those Razorbites can do. I think we'd better stay where we are until we reach the coliseum."

"Grunt isn't afraid of no Razorbites," grumbled Grunt.

"I'm sure you're not," said Torch. "But I certainly don't want them chasing after me."

"Torch is right," said Crank. "We'd better just stay on the racer until we reach the coliseum. Then we can get some fuel and leave Quill and his strange convoy far behind."

"That sounds like a very good idea," agreed Al.

"I still fink we should just punch Bouncer's lights out and help ourselves to some fuel," complained Grunt.

"I do not think Mr Quill would be very happy about that," said Al.

"Ha," laughed Grunt. "What can Quill do? He's a softy and softies can't stop us."

"Perhaps not," said Torch. "But we can't do anything to him either. Everyone knows that robots can't hurt humans."

"Yeah!" agreed Grunt, sitting down on the racer. "Even stinkin' softies like dat Quill. I suppose we just has to wait."

"I do not think we will have long to wait," said Al. "I think I can see the coliseum."

The four robots eagerly peered into the distance, and sure enough, the walls of the coliseum could be seen rising up from the dusty ground of the Wastelands. A scattering of smaller buildings lay on either side of it and the air above was full of spacecraft and land cruisers as they buzzed around.

"It looks busier than I thought," said Torch. "This could get interesting."

The coliseum was a vast building that towered over everything but the mountains themselves, and even they somehow didn't look nearly as impressive or as solid.

Built by the Ancients, thousands of years before, the coliseum had been used as many things in its time. Its huge stone walls offered shelter from the dust storms that ravaged the Wastelands and provided defence against scavengers and other undesirables.

At one end of the coliseum a huge gateway gave access to the central arena and flights of stone steps that led up to seating areas and balconies high above the ground. The doors, once made of wood, had been replaced over the years with blast proof metal.

As Quill's convoy approached the gateway, the blast doors slowly opened and the first of the land cruisers went inside.

"They used this place as a robot prison while they were building the moon station," said Torch. "It's supposed to have been empty since everyone was shipped up there though."

"It doesn't look empty now," said Crank, looking up at the seating.

Groups of spectators were already bustling around trying to find seats that would give the best view of the show. Most of them were robots but Crank also spotted a few aliens from off-world and even a few softies with their robot bodyguards.

"Everyone must be here to watch the travelling show," said Al. "I do hope we get good seats …

it all looks very exciting."

High above the arena floor, wooden cages were hanging from the ends of long lengths of rope. Looking up, Crank could see a row of wooden beams protruding from the very top of the coliseum. Each one had a small pulley wheel attached to it where the rope threaded through. The other ends of the ropes were tied to large metal rings set in the arena floor.

As soon as the convoy was inside the arena, the blast doors closed and Quill's robots set to work. Bouncer jumped to the floor and started directing a small group of robots, shouting at them and pointing up at the wooden cages.

The robot workers scurried around, tripping over each other in their haste to carry out Bouncer's orders.

Crank watched as one of the robots started loosening the rope that was tied to one of the metal floor rings.

The little robot had trouble with the knot at first but eventually managed to work it loose. When the rope was free, the robot wrapped it tightly round its hand and looked up at the wooden cage.

The cage hadn't moved so the little robot gave the rope a gentle tug. There was a faint creaking sound from above as the rope pulled against the old pulley wheel but nothing else happened.

The little robot gave the rope another tug and this time something did happen.

There was a much louder creak from above and the rope suddenly slipped. The wooden cage plummeted down to the floor and the little robot flew up into the air, fastened to the end of the rope.

As the wooden cage hit the floor far below it exploded in a shower of splinters and dust, sending pieces of wood flying in all directions.

"YOU USELESS PIECE OF JUNK," yelled

Bouncer. "I *said* work in twos."

The weight of the cage had been enough to catapult the little robot into the air where it dangled high above the arena floor, but with the cage in splinters there was no longer enough weight on the end of the rope to keep the robot up and it too came crashing to the floor, letting out a shrill, whistling scream as it fell.

The little robot landed in a heap at Bouncer's feet, ribbons of blue smoke snaking out from its joints.

"You worthless little drone," growled Bouncer, grabbing one of the robot's legs.

The other robot workers had stopped what they were doing to watch what was going on. Bouncer turned and roared at them. "This is what will happen to the rest of you if you don't do as you're told."

Bouncer swung the little robot round his head a couple of times as if it were a lasso, then let go, sending it flying through the air where it smashed into one of the wooden cages. The little robot fell down in a shower of wood and dust but was snatched up, before hitting the ground, by one of Quill's Razorbites.

The Razorbite clattered to the ground with its victim and tore it apart with its deadly claws, but the sound of the tearing metal was soon drowned out as the other robots quickly got back to work.

In a few minutes the wooden cages had been lowered to floor and the workers had moved on to other jobs.

"I wonder what they are going to use these for?" said Al, looking at one of the cages.

"I've no idea," said Torch. "But they *were* used as prison cells."

"Really?" said Al, walking into the cage and giving the bars a shake. "I cannot see how they would work as prison cells, they do not seem strong enough."

"They are not very big either," said Crank, joining Al in the cage. "It would be a bit of a squeeze with two of us in here."

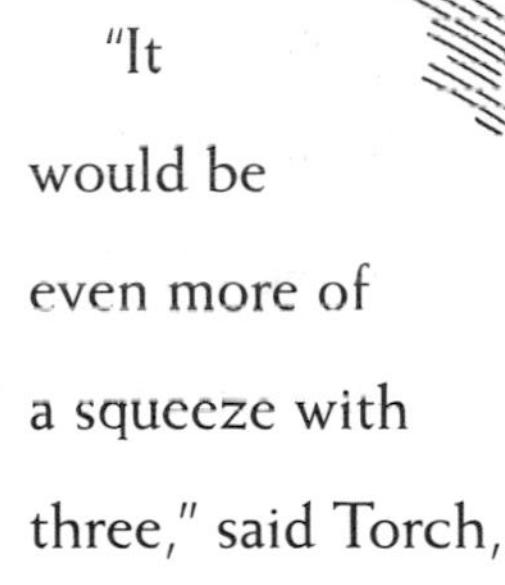

"It would be even more of a squeeze with three," said Torch, getting into the cage. "But this is how it used to be for the robot prisoners that were kept here."

"Thank you for the history lesson," said Quill, slamming the cage door. "And thank you *so* much for making our job easier for us."

The ground suddenly moved beneath the robots' feet as the cage lifted into the air. Torch tried to step back but the cage door blocked his way.

"What are you doing?" yelled Torch.

"*I* am not doing anything," said Quill. "But you'll notice Bouncer is lifting you into the air. Soon you will be high above the arena. Isn't that right, Bouncer?"

"Oh yeah," agreed Bouncer, hoisting the cage into the air. "They'll be dead high."

"Grunt finks you 'ad better let them go," growled Grunt, moving towards Quill.

"I think not," said Quill, smiling at Grunt. "And *you* will do as I say."

Grunt was puzzled for a moment. He wasn't

used to people smiling at him like that. He was used to people doing what he told them. But it didn't matter – he knew what to do.

It was time to stop being polite.

Clapping one huge hand on to Quill's shoulder, Grunt squeezed.

Quill should have fallen to the floor, screaming in agony, but instead, he laughed. Grunt stared at his hand for a moment, wondering what was wrong. Then he clenched the fingers of his other hand into a giant fist and punched Quill in the face.

Grunt's huge fist stopped a centimetre from the end of Quill's nose.

"You can't hurt me," laughed Quill. "Robots aren't allowed to hurt humans ... had you forgotten that?"

Grunt groaned. He *had* forgotten. Quill was a softy, and robots were programmed not to hurt softies. It was one of the laws built into every robot.

Torch had been right, they couldn't do anything to Quill.

Then, like a sledgehammer, Quill's gloved fist sent him crashing to the floor. Blue sparks danced over Grunt's body and his joints felt as though they had been turned to stone. Grunt just had time to wonder how a softy could punch so hard before everything went dark.

8

When Grunt's eyes opened again, everything was *still* dark, but looking round he saw light coming through a hole set against one wall. A thin, pale glow of light running along the ground suggested it might be a door. Grunt stood up to get a better look and found that metal chains had been fastened around his wrists and ankles.

The ankle chains snapped like old rope as Grunt walked forwards, and one of the wrist chains broke easily as he crunched it between his teeth. The last chain was much tougher and Grunt had to grip it in both hands, placing one foot against the wall and pulling as hard he could.

There was a rough grinding sound and Grunt staggered back as the chain came away from the wall, bringing the huge stone block it was fastened to along with it.

With the stone block dragging behind him, Grunt walked across to the door and peered through the hole. The room on the other side was round with more metal doors set around the outsides. It was also full of robots. Most of them were small workers like the ones he'd seen earlier lowering the wooden cages, but some were much bigger, and they *all* carried weapons. Some had clubs and pieces of chain but others carried electro-lances, long poles with a spark of electricity flickering at the end.

Standing on a raised platform at the other side of the room were Quill and his bodyguard, Bouncer. Quill was talking and smiling at everyone, though Grunt couldn't hear much of what was being said as the robots were shouting and cheering. Only a few words reached him – *freedom, fight, death* and *slaves*. None of it made much sense but Grunt didn't care. He'd had enough waiting around and being polite. It was time to find his friends and get out of here.

Grunt opened the metal door with his foot and sent it crashing to the floor, partly squashing a little robot beneath it. Grunt finished the job by walking over the fallen door and into the round room. Dust and chunks of stone rained down on to his head and back from the ruined doorway but Grunt ignored it as he strode towards the platform where Quill and Bouncer were standing.

"Destroy him," said Quill, stepping further back on to the platform.

The robots charged at Grunt, attacking him with clubs, metal bars and pieces of chain, but Grunt was ready for them. Three robots fell to floor beneath the weight of the stone block as Grunt swung it round on the end of its chain.

Another flew back against the wall in a shower of sparks when his huge fist caught it on the chin.

Blows rained down from all sides as the robots attacked, but Grunt swatted them away like flies. Soon, the room was hissing and buzzing with the crackle of electricity as most of the attackers were knocked to the ground.

"ENOUGH!" shouted Quill, clapping his hands together.

Grunt stood in the middle of the room surrounded by all that was left of his attackers. In one hand he held a robot's leg he'd been using to bash the others with and from the other dangled the huge stone block.

In one sudden movement, the bigger robots from round the outside of the room stepped forward and lowered their electro-lances.

Grunt swung the huge stone block in a deadly arc above his head and brought it crashing down on to the one closest to him. The robot crumpled and folded like a concertina as the block drove it down to the floor and the weapon it had been holding dropped to the ground, a spark of electric charge flickering out from the end.

The spark touched Grunt's foot and the charge crackled and danced up his leg, sending shivers through his joints and circuits. His leg shook uncontrollably and Grunt let out a cry of rage as another stab of electricity jolted into his back, then another in his arm. Grunt thrashed around madly, trying to defend himself from the new attackers, but it was no use ... As the electric charge danced across his body his legs gave way and he fell to his knees.

The last thing Grunt saw was Quill's smiling face as he fell forwards on to the floor, a wisp of blue smoke curling out from the joints around his neck.

From their cage high above the arena, Crank, Al and Torch had watched as the robot prisoners were taken from the land cruisers and put into the other cages.

The six Razorbites had buzzed and rattled around in the air for a while, leaping from cage to cage, snapping their jaws and clicking their claws until the last of the robots had been moved. Then they settled high up on the coliseum walls like vultures, watching everything that was going on.

The seats around the coliseum were filling up quickly with chattering spectators, and land cruisers, spacecraft and drop ships were bringing more and more people by the minute.

High above the arena the sound of the crowd was just a loud babble of noise which grew louder and louder as they grew impatient for things to start.

"I can not believe we are being kept in a cage like these criminals," said Al, looking across at the other cages hanging in the air.

"I don't believe these robots are criminals at all," said Torch. "They are all just robots like us that have been picked up or stolen by Quill."

"There must be some way out of here," said Crank, shaking the wooden bars of the cage.

"I could carefully burn through some of the bars," suggested Torch, fiddling with one of the dials on his arm.

"No!" cried Al. "You will set fire to the whole thing and send us crashing to the ground."

Suddenly, the cage jolted as the rope was given a sharp tug. Looking down, the three friends could see Bouncer untying the rope from the metal ring that was holding it.

"I think we're going down," said Torch, as a cheer went up from the crowd.

"It is about time too," complained Al. "I am getting fed up with hanging around up here."

"You might change your mind when we get down there," said Torch. "I've got a really bad feeling about this."

The three robots gripped the bars and peered out at the crowd as the cage was slowly lowered to the ground.

"**Ladies and gentlemen**," boomed Quill's voice. "**You've travelled a great distance for today's entertainment ... and now your wait is almost over**."

A loud, roaring cheer went up from the crowd then died away as Quill spoke again

"**Fresh from their escape from the prison ships of Ganymede 6, I bring you the deadliest trio of killer robots ever to walk the earth**."

The crowd hissed and booed at the mention of the killer robots and Crank, Al and Torch looked around in fear.

"Killer robots?" said Crank. "We're not killer robots."

The wooden cage stopped when it touched the floor and Bouncer sneered at the three friends.

"It's showtime," said Bouncer, opening the cage door. "You're free to go."

"*What?*" said Crank. "You're letting us go? … I don't understand."

"Of course," said Bouncer, smiling, "you just have to survive. But you'll have to do better than your big stupid friend."

While Crank, Al and Torch left the wooden cage, Bouncer began lowering the others to the ground.

"What did he mean … *we'll have to do better than our big stupid friend?*" asked Crank.

"I hope he does not mean Grunt," said Al "I think we should find him and get out of here."

"I don't think it's going to be *that* easy," said Torch.

As the three friends walked across the arena floor the crowd booed, hissed and began stamping their feet.

"What's the matter with them?" asked Crank.

"They think we're killer robots," said Torch,

ducking as something whizzed past his head.

"HEY!" he cried. "Someone threw something at me."

"It's a spanner," said Crank picking it up off the floor.

"**Ladies and gentlemen**," boomed Quill's voice. "**The first of them has found a weapon … Now watch as these robots fight to the death**."

Another loud cheer went up from the crowd and Crank looked at the spanner in his hand.

"*A weapon?*" said Crank. "What's he talking about? I've not got a weapon."

"And what was that about fighting to the death?" asked Al.

"Of course!" said Torch. "I've got it. Thousands of years ago, gladiators used to fight in this coliseum. Many of them were escaped slaves who fought in the hope of winning their freedom."

"But we don't want to fight," said Crank.

"No," agreed Torch. "But *they* might …"

The other cages had been lowered to the ground and the robots inside them had all found weapons. Now they were walking towards the three friends with metal bars, clubs and pieces of chain.

"Oh dear," said Al. "This does not look good at all."

"Perhaps we could try talking to them," suggested Crank.

"Good idea," said Al. "Why not try those two?"

Two robots were standing right behind Crank. One had a large metal bar and the other was swinging a long chain around its head.

"You're making a big mistake," explained Crank, as the robot with the metal bar came towards him.

Thwack, the bar hit him on the side of his head, almost knocking it off his shoulders. As Crank staggered back the second robot lashed out with the metal chain. It flicked out like a striking snake but Crank managed to lift his arm to protect himself and the chain wrapped itself around it.

"Aha," said Crank, triumphantly pulling at the chain.

The robot snarled and tugged back as hard as it could. There was a loud pop and Crank's arm fell to the floor. The two robots howled with laughter and started coming forwards again with their weapons.

"I really think we should talk about this," said Crank, snatching his broken arm up from the floor. "We shouldn't be fighting ... we should be friends."

"There are no friends here," snarled one of the robots. "Quill says only the winner will be given their freedom."

"Sorry to interrupt," said Al, "but did you say *only* the winner?"

"Of course," snarled the robot. "One winner. It's a fight to the death. Are you lot stupid or what?"

"But there are two of you," said Al. "And if there can only be *one* winner ..."

The two robots stood and thought about this for a moment, then the one with the metal bar came to a decision.

Thwack, the bar hit the second robot and sent its head spinning through the air. Sparks flew from the robot's neck and it staggered back, crashing to the floor.

In a matter of seconds the air was filled with the crash and clatter of metal hitting metal and the whole arena became one giant battle with every robot fighting for themselves.

The crowds of spectators cheered louder than ever as the fighting in the arena increased and robots fell to the floor, battered and broken.

Crank, Al and Torch ducked and dodged their way towards the edge of the arena, hoping to find a way out.

"This way," suggested Al. "I am sure no one will notice us. The crowd seem rather busy at the moment."

Crank thought Al might be right. There seemed to be a disturbance in the crowd and people were jumping around in their seats, shouting, as something big and silver ran between them.

"Come on," said Torch, helping Crank up the wall. "Let's go."

Torch had just turned back to help Al when

something landed on the ground between them.

It was Bouncer.

"Where do you think you're going?" growled Bouncer, grabbing Crank's leg and pulling him off the wall. "I knew you lot would be trouble," he snarled, lifting Crank into the air.

"Let go," demanded Crank, waving his broken arm at Bouncer, "or you'll be sorry."

"Oh dear," said Bouncer. "I'd better let you go then." And with that, Bouncer swung Crank above his head and let him go.

"Arrrrgh!" yelled Crank, as he flew high up into the air above the arena.

"Now," sneered Bouncer. "Which one of you tin-heads is next?"

As the big robot came towards him, Torch adjusted one of the dials on his arm.

"This is why they call me Torch!" he shouted … and a small jet of blue flame came out from his wrist.

"Is that the best you can do?" laughed Bouncer, picking up a piece of chain.

Torch frantically twiddled the dials again and the small jet of flame erupted into a huge ball of fire which engulfed Bouncer from head to toe.

The big robot staggered back, waving his arms around to shield himself from the flame.

The crowd roared with delight at seeing the big robot ablaze and chants of "burn, burn, burn," filled the air.

"Ha!" cried Torch triumphantly. "*This* is the best I can do … This is for Crank and Grunt … You'll wish you'd never messed with us."

As the flame died away, Torch and Al were horrified to find Bouncer still standing. Smoke was rising from his head and body, most of his paint had peeled off and he didn't look happy. But apart from that, he didn't seem to have been damaged at all.

"You've ruined my suit ..." growled Bouncer, looking at his peeling paint. "But you're right. I'm not going to mess with you any more. I'm going to squash you into the floor."

"Crush-em, crush-em, crush-em," yelled the crowd.

Bouncer stepped forward and made a grab for

Torch, but as he did there was a sudden flash of silver and something big and heavy, with razor-sharp teeth and claws, flew out of the crowd and landed on him.

"It's Scamp!" cried Torch, still backing away.

Bouncer howled with rage as he staggered around, trying desperately to get the robo-dog off his back, but the botweiler wouldn't be moved. There was a loud crunch as the robo-dog's teeth tore through metal and Bouncer let out a loud cry as he fell to his knees.

Torch and Al had seen what the big robo-dog did to its victims and they didn't want to see it again. As the two friends turned away in search of Crank the air was filled with the sound of tearing metal.

Bouncer wouldn't be bothering *them*, or any other robots, again.

High above the crowded arena, Crank clung to the remains of one of the old wooden cages. Every time he moved, the wood creaked and groaned, threatening to collapse at any moment and send him crashing to the floor far below.

After Bouncer let go, Crank had flown into the air like a rag doll. Up above the crowd he went, spinning and twisting through the air, higher and higher.

It was going to be a long drop back down to the floor and Crank hadn't wanted to see it so he closed his eyes. Then something unexpected happened.

He stopped.

Looking up, Crank had found his broken arm had got caught in the bottom of one of the old wooden cages.

Crank hardly dared to move in case his arm came loose, then, very slowly, he started to pull himself up to the beam above.

Clambering on top of the wooden beam, Crank flopped on to his back and looked up at the sky.

"I'm impressed," said a voice from behind him.

Crank jumped with surprise, nearly dropping his broken arm and falling off the beam.

Quill was standing at the other end of the wooden beam with an evil grin on his face.

"Pulling yourself on to that beam with only one arm. Poor Bouncer would have been very disappointed that the Razorbites didn't snatch you out of the air like they were supposed to do."

As Quill stepped out on to the wooden beam it creaked and groaned under his weight.

Crank turned and tried to crawl away, but Quill quickly grabbed his foot.

A loud cheer went up from the crowd below as some of them noticed the action that was taking place high above them.

"Now, now," said Quill, lifting Crank into the air. "We don't want you falling off and hurting yourself, do we? Bouncer was right," he continued, holding Crank out over the arena.

"You lot *were* trouble and we *should* have left you to rust in the Wastelands."

"You could just let us go now," suggested Crank. "We'll be out of here before you know it."

Hanging upside down, Crank knew that if he

fell from here there wouldn't be much left of him. But there wasn't much he could do about it – his fate was in Quill's hands.

Then he saw something …

something was moving behind Quill.

"Perhaps you *should* have left us," said Crank. "But it's too late for that now."

"Too late?" said Quill. "It's never too late."

"Yes it is," said Crank. "You can drop me if you want, but that won't be the end of it. My friends will come after you."

"Drop you?" said Quill. "I'm not going to drop you."

In one quick movement, Quill threw Crank up into the air and caught him again, this time gripping his head between his hands. It felt as though his head was being crushed and Crank couldn't help being amazed at how strong Quill was for a softy.

"So!" laughed Quill, "what are your friends going to do about this?"

Hanging over the arena, Crank could feel Quill's powerful hands holding his head in a vice-like grip. He could hear his neck joints creaking under the strain of holding the weight of his body. Quill wouldn't *need* to drop him because if he stayed like this much longer his neck joints would snap and his body would plummet to the ground.

Crank desperately kicked and punched, but it was no use. He couldn't even touch Quill.

"Is that the best you can do?" Quill sneered.

"Yes," squeaked Crank. "But my friend could do better."

Quill frowned. "What friend?" he said.

"Allo!" said Grunt.

Quill looked puzzled for a moment then looked round and saw Grunt standing behind him.

"*You!*" cried Quill. "But you were destroyed."

"It take more than a few sparks to finish old Grunt," said Grunt, grabbing Quill and pulling him back.

Quill's ancient coat ripped, leaving Grunt with a fistful of filthy, rotting fur as Quill himself staggered backwards, slipping on the wooden beam and letting go of Crank at the same time.

Grunt dived forwards, just managing to catch hold of Crank's broken arm and stop him falling.

Quill howled with rage as he got to his feet, tearing the remains of the old coat from his body and throwing it down to the ground far below. A shower of grubs and bugs fell through the air with it and more of them scurried around his body where raw skin met metal.

"He's a cyborg!" cried Crank in disgust.

"Dat's right," said Grunt. "Part softy and part robot. Grunt knew he wasn't no real softy. Softies can't punch like dat."

"You're not as stupid as you sound," said Quill, and clapped his hands together three times. "But it won't do you any good. You'll never escape from here."

"Oh no?" snarled Grunt. "Who's gonna to stop us den?"

A faint but familiar sound made Crank look round.

"RAZORBITES!" he shouted. "RUN!"

Grunt took one look at the Razorbites as they rattled and clattered up the side of the coliseum and ran after Crank as fast as his legs would carry him.

The two robots bounded down the huge stone steps that led from the top of the coliseum, past the cheering crowd. Running past Crank,

Grunt picked his friend up in one huge hand and carried him down with him so they that were on the ground in no time.

As they ran across the arena floor towards Torch and Al, a Razorbite landed between them, its deadly claws clicking and snapping in the air like knives.

Before Grunt reached it there was a blur of movement as Scamp leaped on to the Razorbite, growling and snarling.

The insect-like robot let out a loud squeal as the robo-dog's teeth tore through its metal body and ripped at its insides. Claws snapped and teeth clashed together as the two robot creatures fought.

"Good boy, Scamp," cried Grunt as the robo-dog left the broken Razorbite and ran alongside him.

Catching up with Torch and Al, the friends charged through the blast doors that had been opened by other escaping robots and out into the Wastelands once more. The air behind them was filled with the clatter and rattle of claws as the five remaining Razorbites followed them.

All that remained of Quill's convoy was a couple of badly damaged land cruisers – the rest of them were just clouds of dust in the distance.

Their only hope seemed to be a single space-craft sitting close to the coliseum. Its loading ramp was still down and someone was getting on board.

At the sight of the four robots the figure hurried on to the craft and the air filled with the whine of engines as they started to warm up.

"It's leaving," cried Crank. "Quick."

Clouds of dust rose up below the craft as its launch engines fired for take-off, but luckily, the loading ramp was still open.

Torch reached the ramp first and raced up it and into the spacecraft, closely followed by Crank, Al and Grunt.

"Dat was a close one," said Grunt, as the loading ramp started closing behind them. "Dem Razorbites is nasty."

Then Grunt crashed to the floor as something hit him in the chest.

There was a clatter of metal claws on the floor of the spacecraft and razor-sharp teeth snapped together in front of Grunt's face.

"Hur, hur, hur," laughed Grunt, pushing the robo-dog off him. "You big softy, Scamp. It's

good to see you too."

There was a loud roar of engines from outside as the spacecraft took to the air, leaving the Razorbites and the coliseum far behind it.

"Whose spacecraft *is* this?" asked Torch.

"I've no idea," said Crank. "I thought you knew."

"No," said Torch. "But it did seem to be waiting for us."

"Perhaps it will take us to Robotika," Al suggested.

"Oh dear," said Crank. "I'm getting a bad feeling about this."

Behind them, the door to the flight deck opened with a grinding squeal and a tall, thin robot stepped through it and smiled at the four friends.

"Welcome aboard the *Starship Terrapin*," said the tall, thin robot. "I'm Maximus Bullwart, chief scout for the world-famous powerball team, the Iron City Eagles … and this is your lucky day."

The End

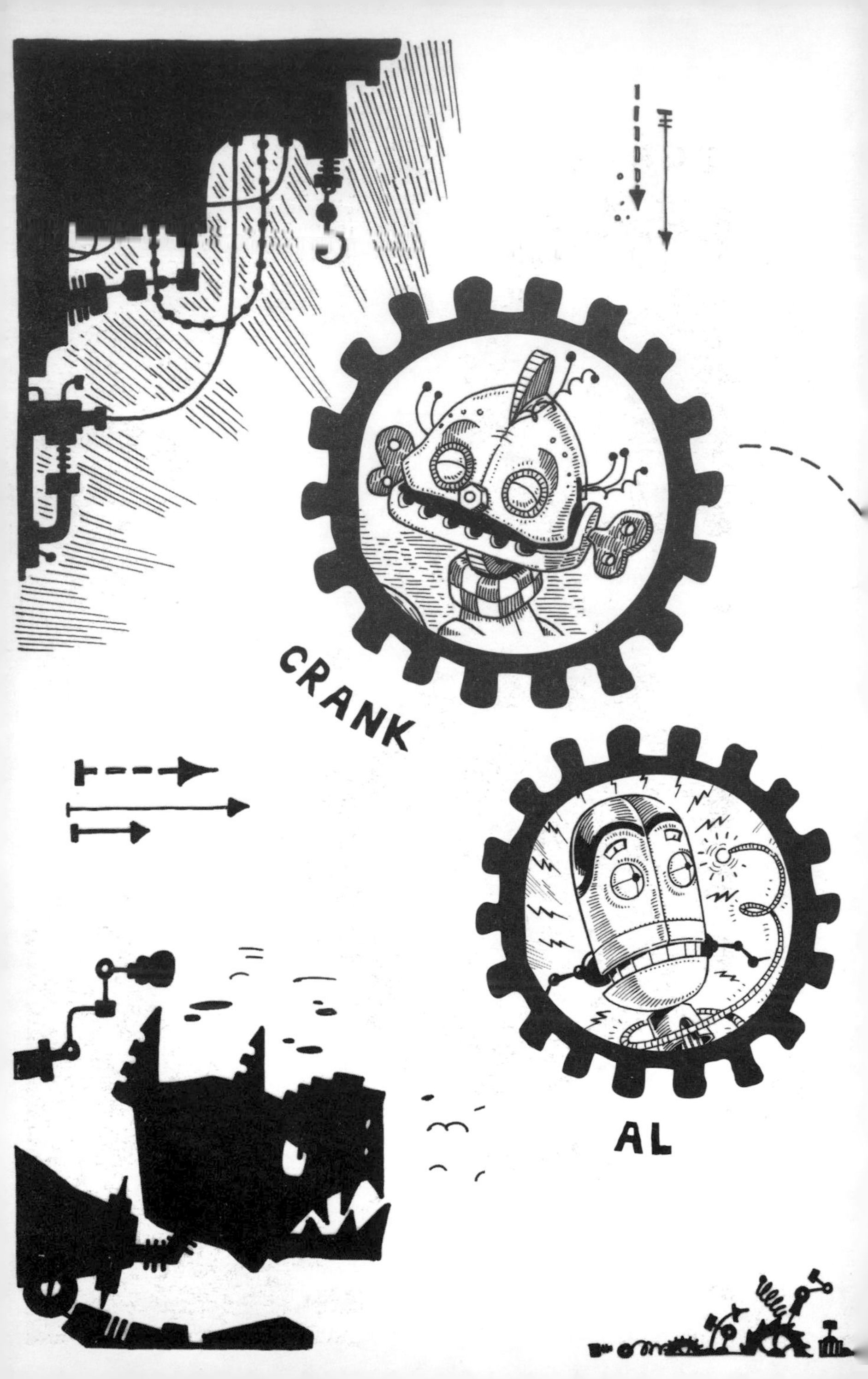
CRANK
AL

TORCH
GRUNT

book 4

Powerball

"It's good to have you on the team," said Avatar, smiling at the four friends. "We need some new players."

"Huh!" growled the other Iron City Eagle behind her – a big old robot with dents and scratches all over his head and body. He glared at Crank and the others for a moment before shaking his head in disgust.

"What we need are *real* players," he said. "Not a bunch of tin cans that have never even *seen* a powerball game."

"I've *seen* lots of powerball games," said Crank, huffily.

"Yes," said Al. "And I have *heard* all about them too."

"You've *heard* about them?" cried the big robot. "*Oh well... there's nothing for us to worry about then, is there?*"

"All right, Flint. That's enough," said Avatar. "I'm sure they'll do their best."

"Yeah, well," said Flint, scowling. "Let's just hope that their best is good enough."

DAMIAN HARVEY
ROBO-RUNNERS
Powerball

DAMIAN HARVEY

lives in Blackpool with his wife and three daughters, their four cats, a horde of guinea pigs, a tank full of fish and a quirky imagination.

He loves music, movies, reading, swimming, walking, cheese and ice cream – but not always at the same time.

Before realising how much fun he could have writing and making things up he worked as a lifeguard, had a job in a boring office and once saved the galaxy from invading vampire robots (though none of these were as exciting as they sound).

Damian now spends lots of time in front of his computer but loves getting out to visit schools and libraries to share stories, talk about writing and get people excited about books.